MW00396978

IS
IT
THE
SAME
FOR
YOU?

THE INDIA LIST

# IS IT THE SAME FOR YOU?

*Illustrations by Priya Sebastian*
*Text by Neha Singh*

Seagull
BOOKS

LONDON NEW YORK CALCUTTA

**Seagull Books, 2019**

Illustrations © Priya Sebastian, 2019

Text © Neha Singh, 2019

This compilation © Seagull Books, 2019

ISBN   978 0 8574 2 696 3

**British Library Cataloguing-in-Publication Data**

A catalogue record for this book is available from the British Library

Designed and typeset by Sunandini Banerjee, Seagull Books

Printed and bound by Hyam Enterprises, Calcutta, India

*For Armin,*
*The answer to your question from long ago*
~Priya


*For Asifa Bano,*
*whose eyes sparkled like the stars on a moonless night*
~Neha

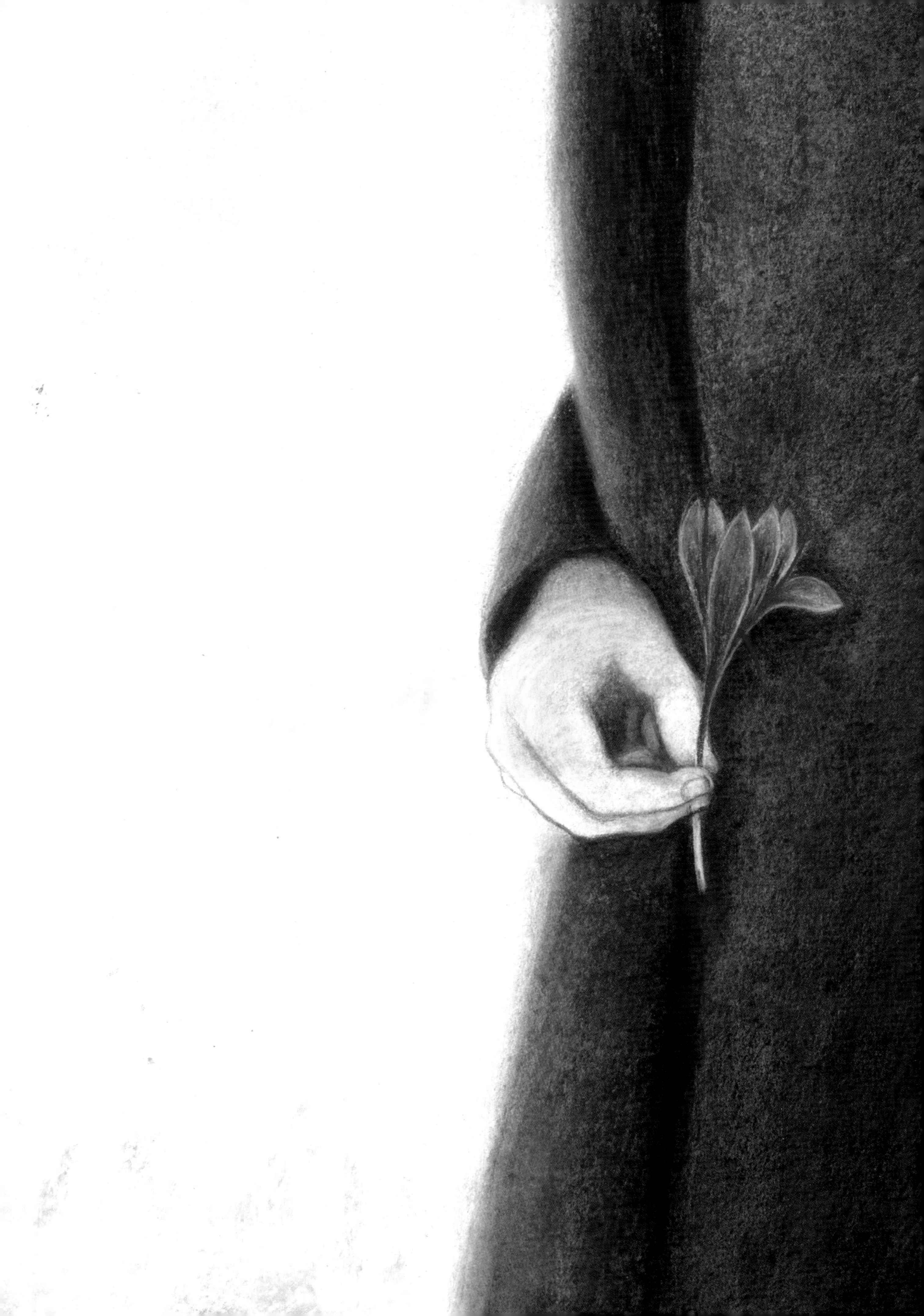

The day they found my brother with a blood stain,
I found one on my kurta too,
but no one noticed mine.

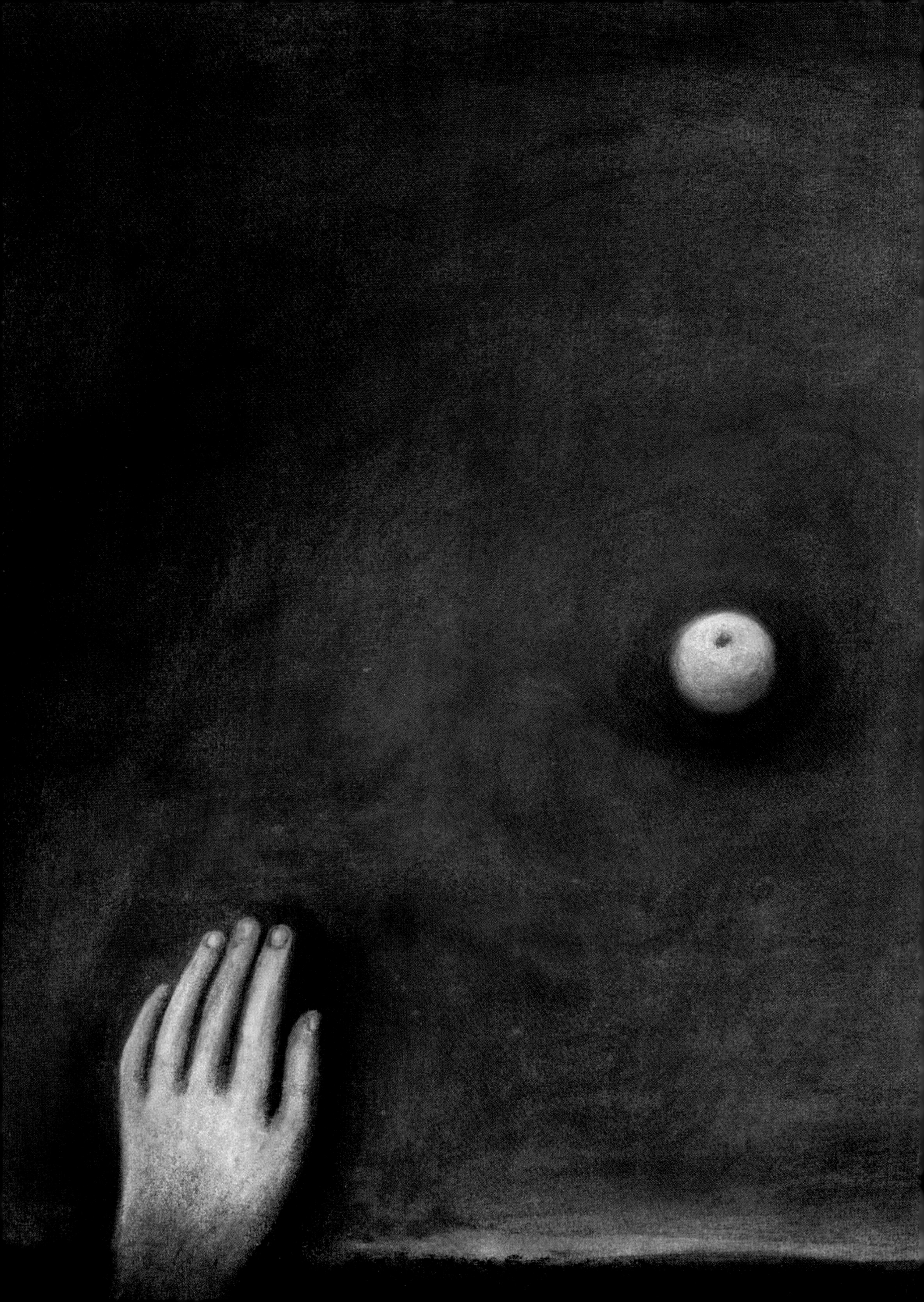

I feel hungry all the time these days.


Today Mother was out all day,
marching with the others in the streets.
I ate up everything in the kitchen.
Hopefully tomorrow won't be a curfew and
we can buy vegetables.

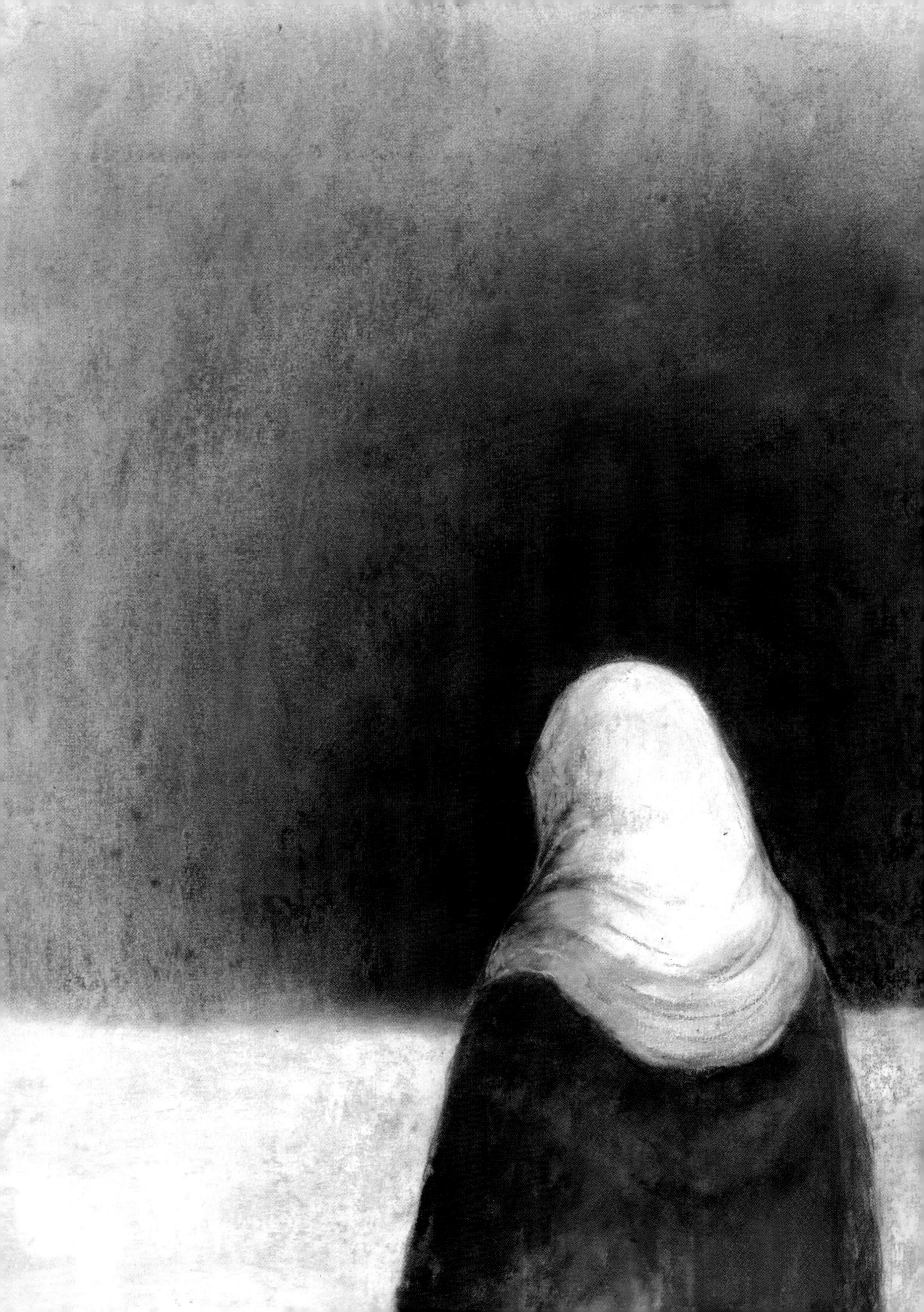

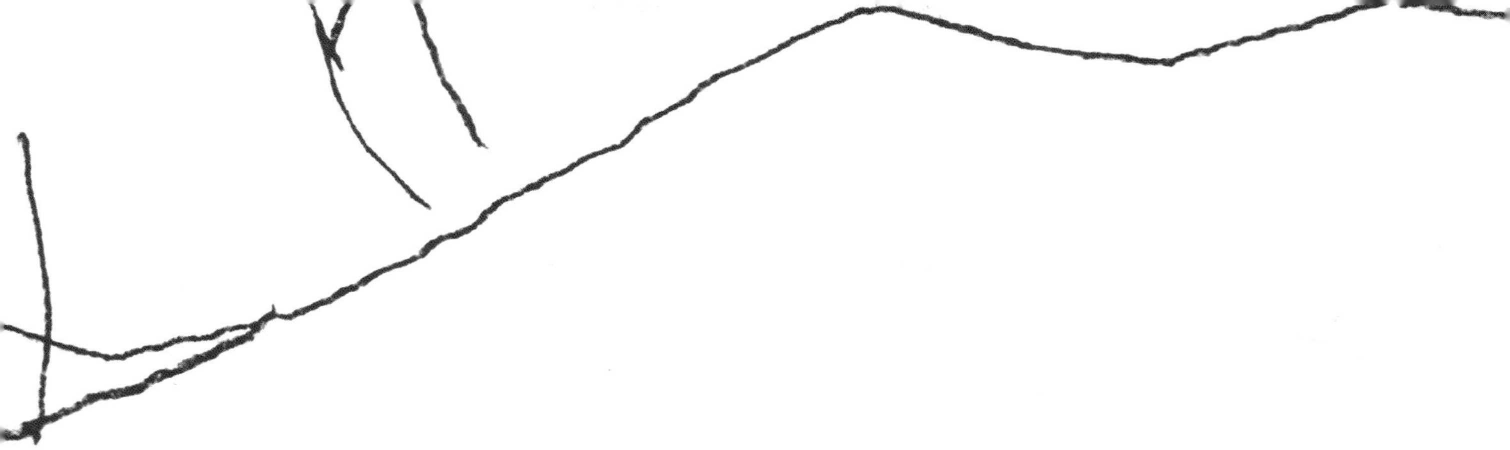

One day, on my way to school, there was a random search by the men in uniform. This is usual for us. But the man in uniform put his hands on my chest and then kept them there longer than usual.

I wanted to scream, but the queue was long and I was late for school, so I quietly left.

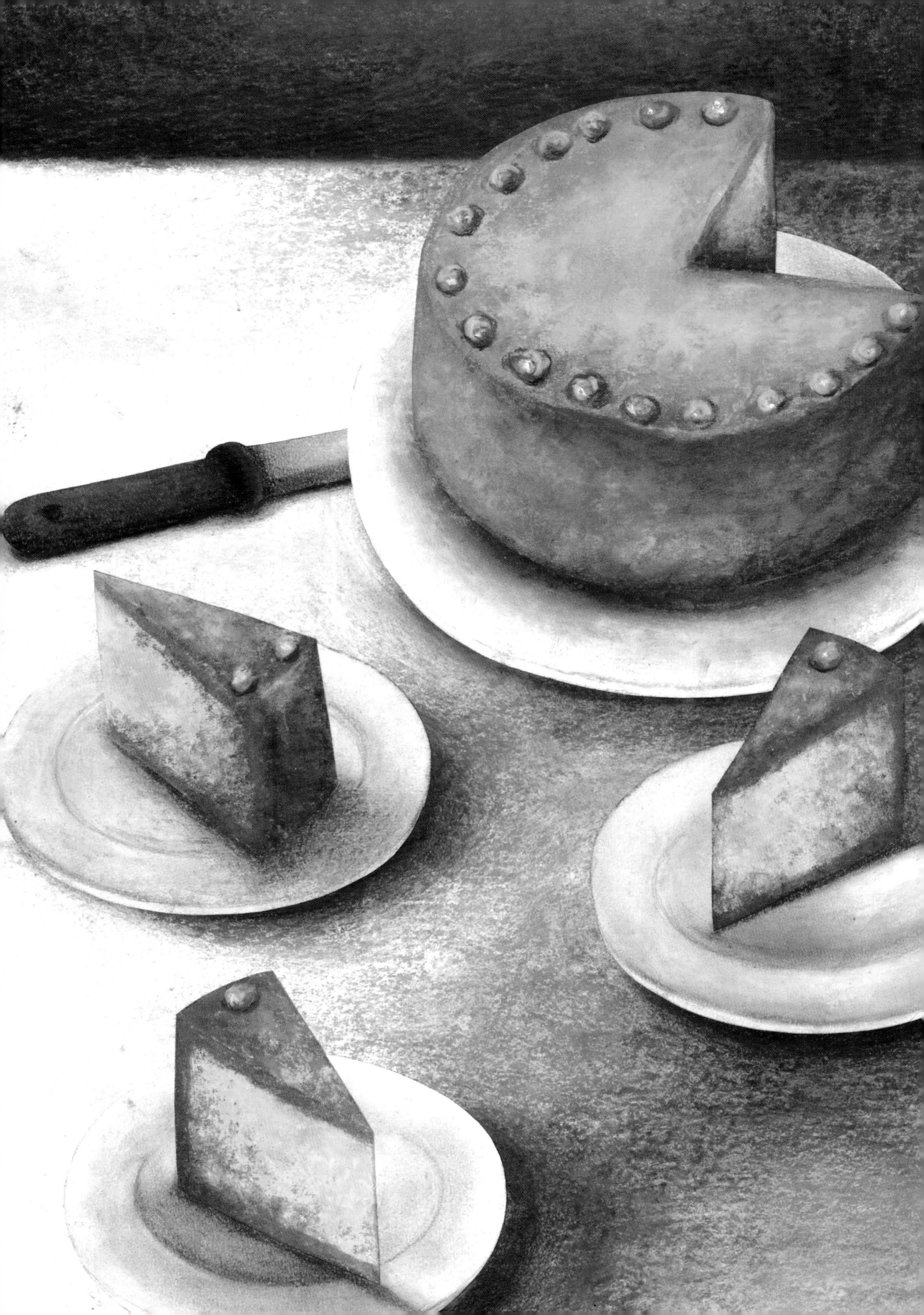

Tonight was fun—my girlfriends stayed over for the
night after my birthday party. They hadn't planned to,
but a curfew was declared, so they couldn't go home.

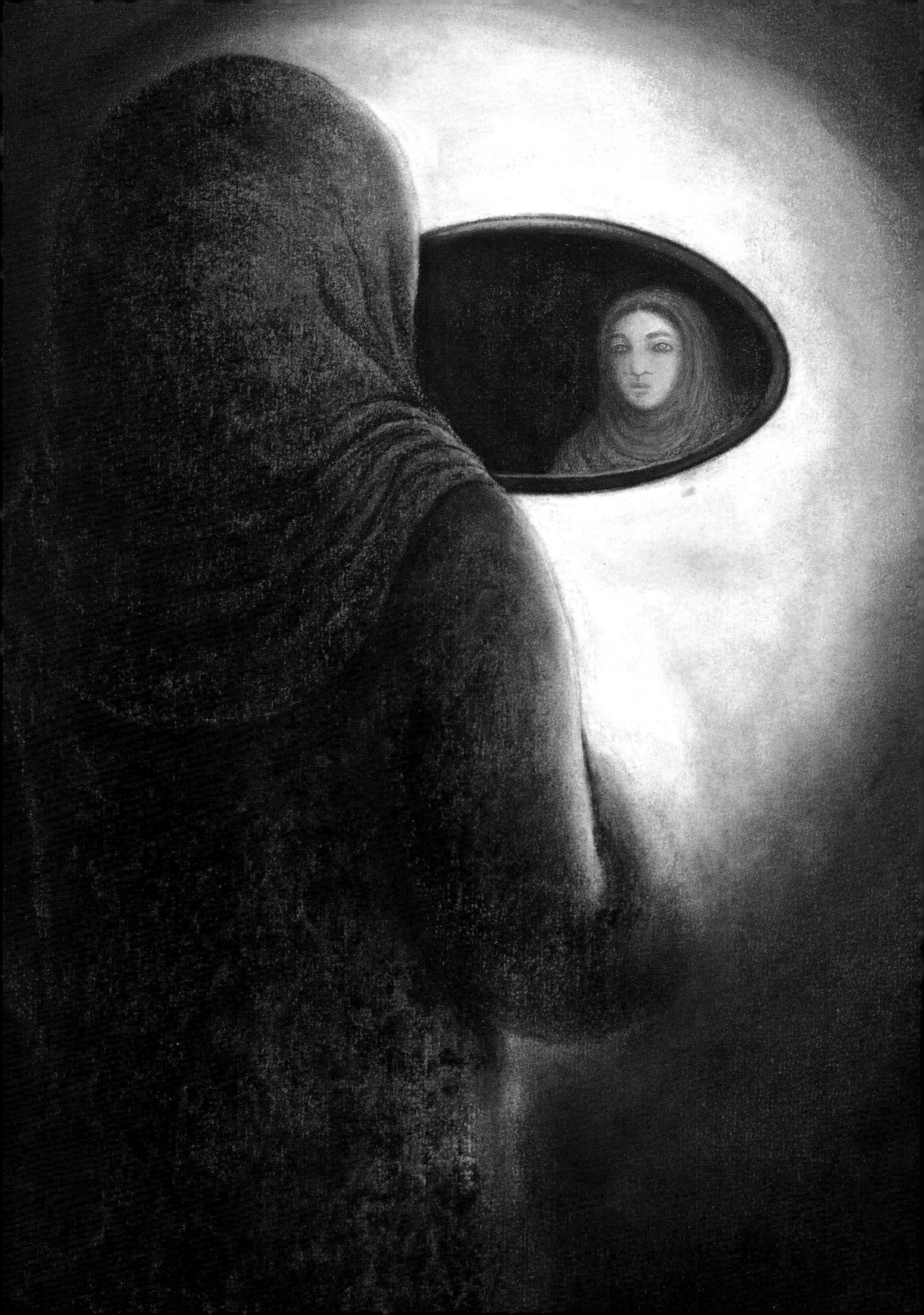

Since I started my period, I have to wear a scarf.
I looked at myself in the mirror.
I had mixed feelings about it.

That same night my cousin returned home after six months. He had been in hiding. He was wearing a scarf too. But I could never ask him what his feelings were about it. Mother cried, Aunt cried, Grandmother cried. I cried too, for him, but also for myself.

He left the next morning.

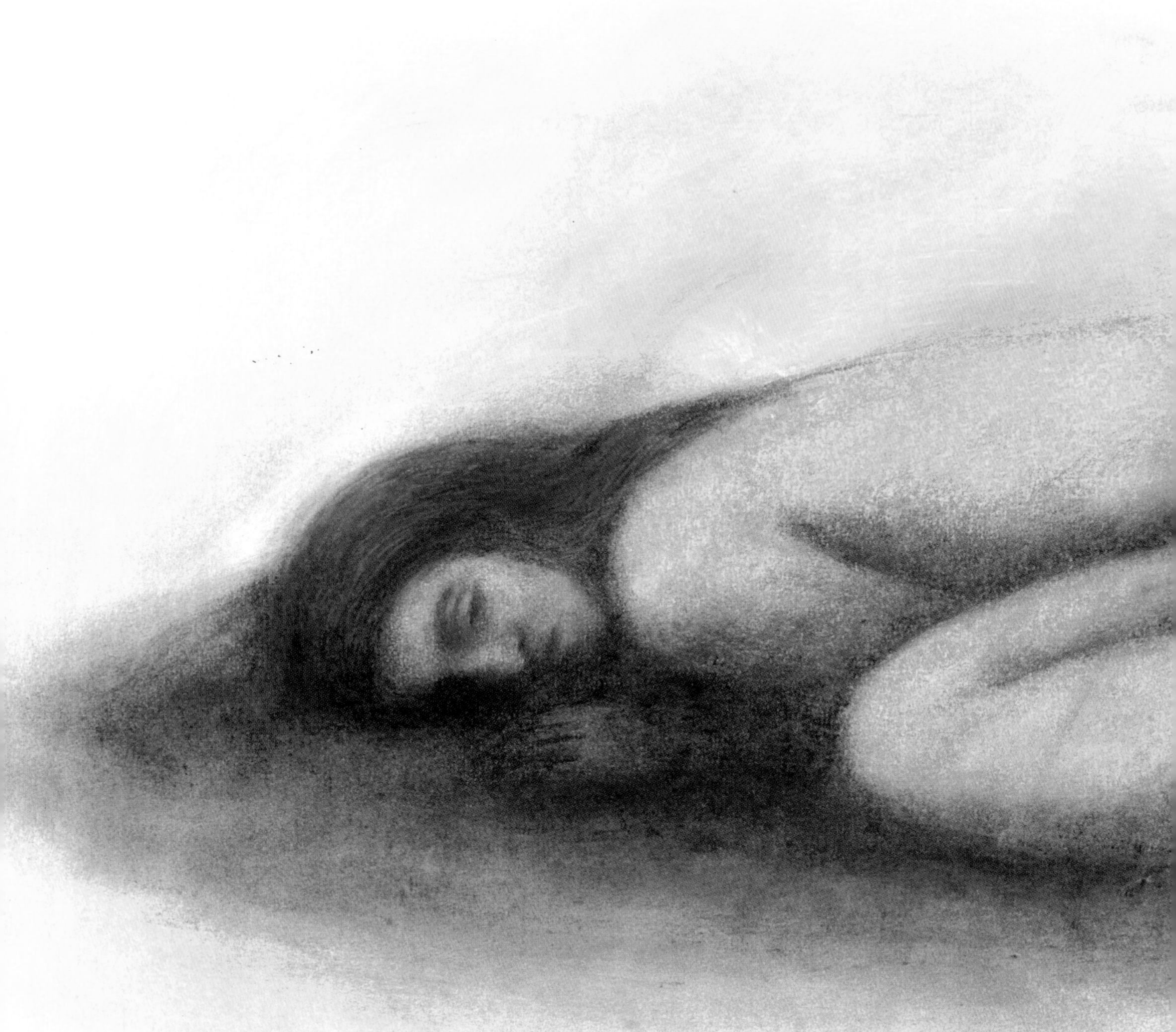

I like a boy.

I have been missing him a lot.

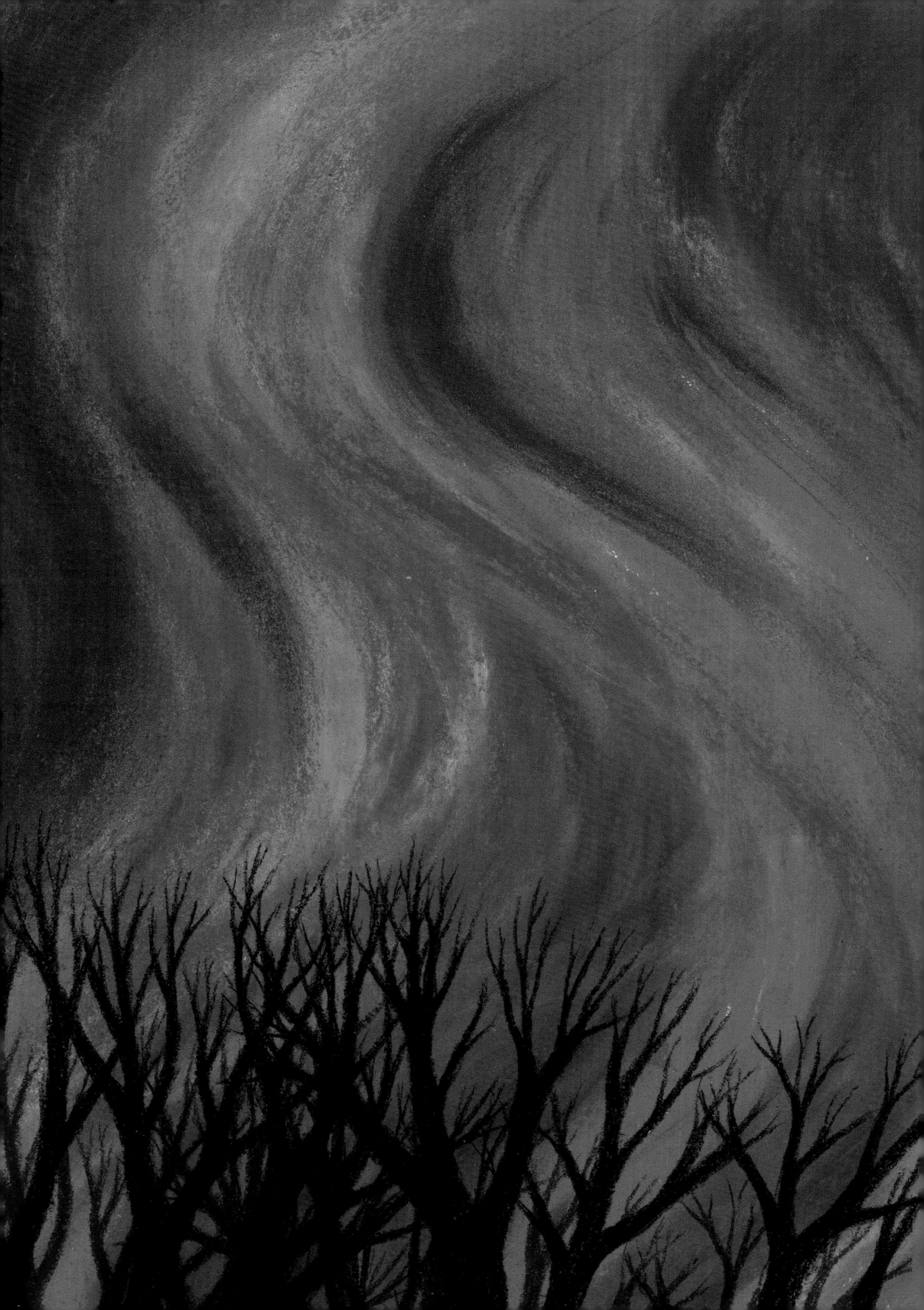

When it's exploding outside, Mother and I
sing songs of hope and youth even louder,
to drown out the noise.

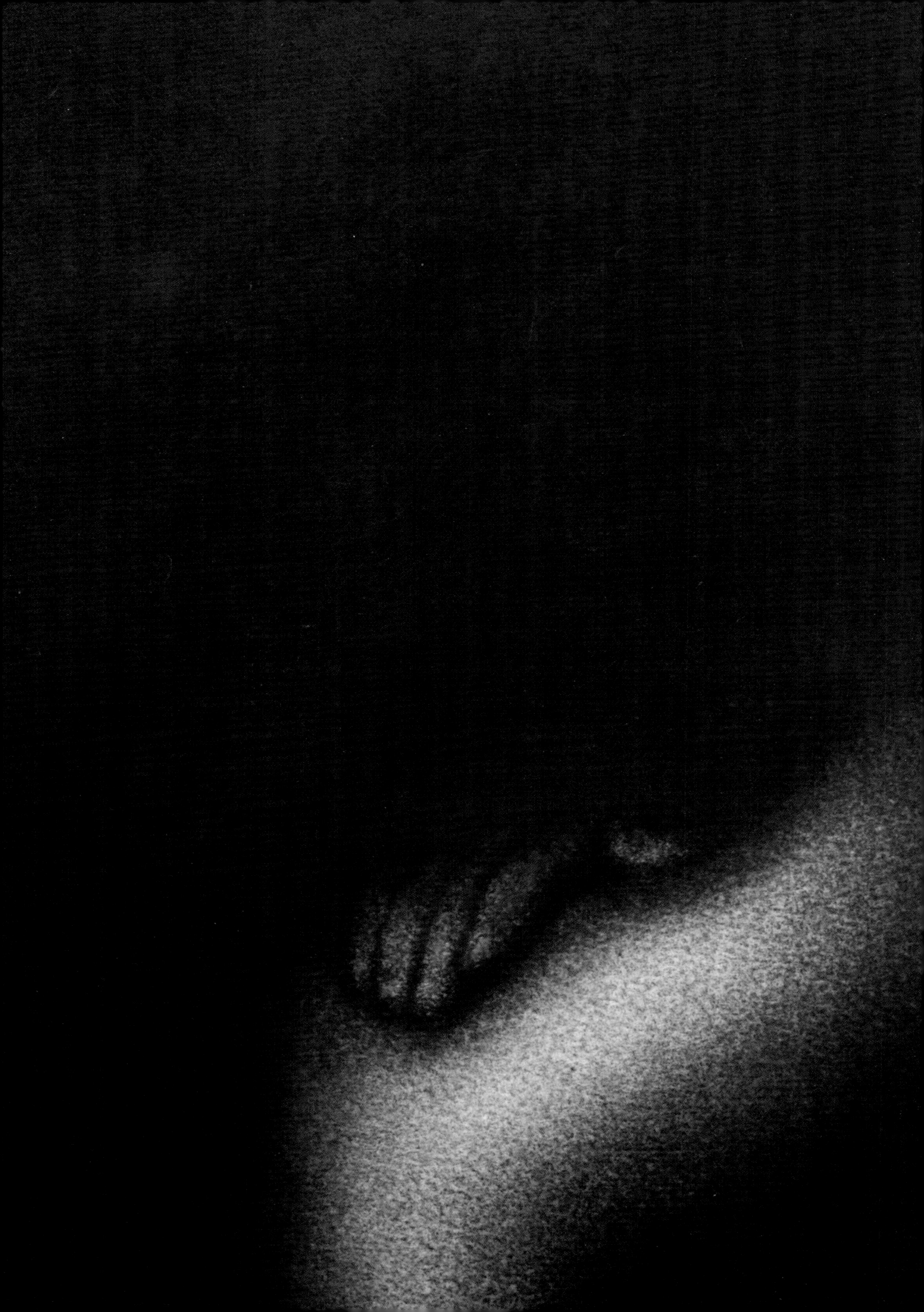

Is this the smell from my new hairy, sweaty armpits or just the usual smell of tear gas and burning tyres?

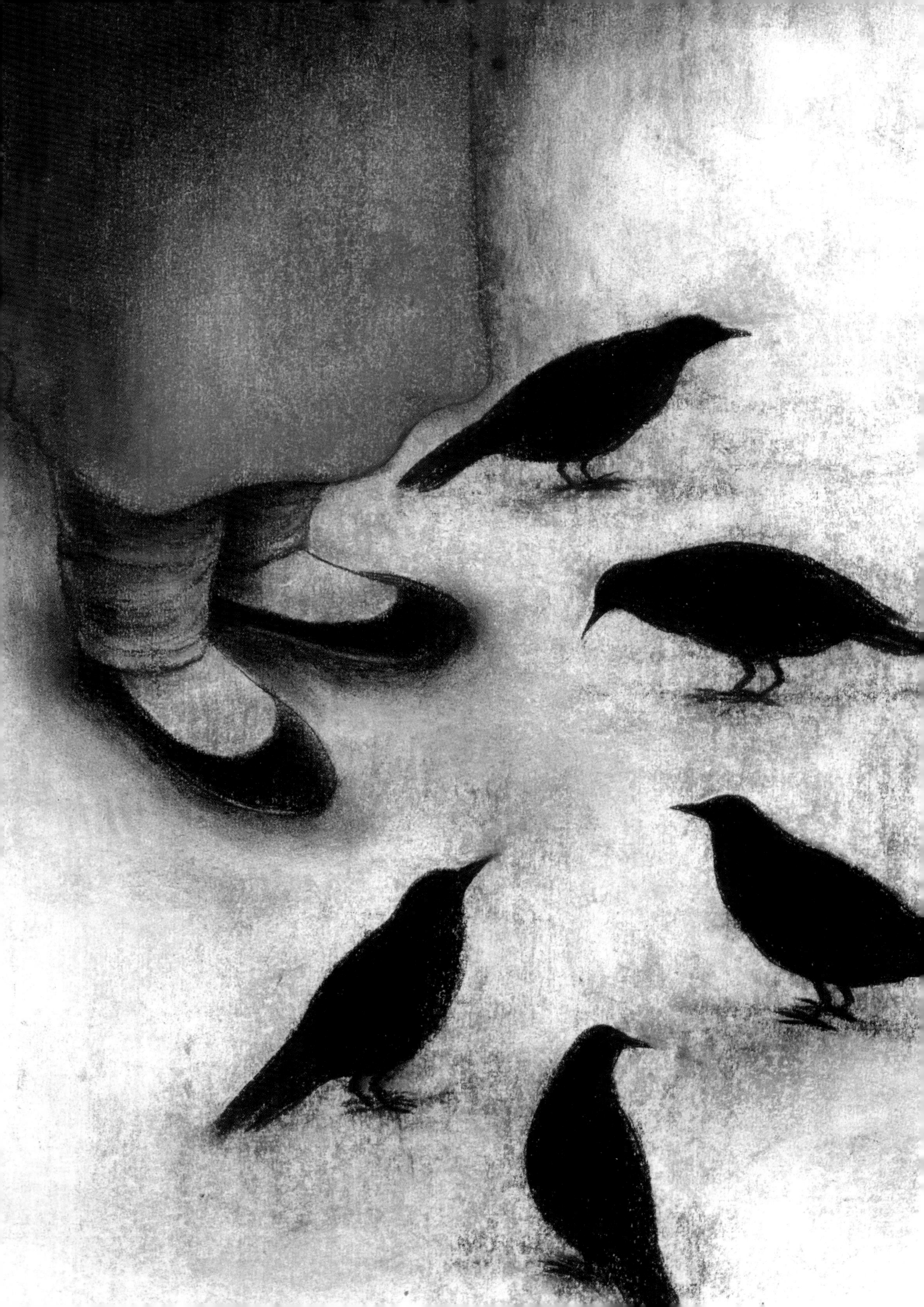

I don't have to fight for the football any more.

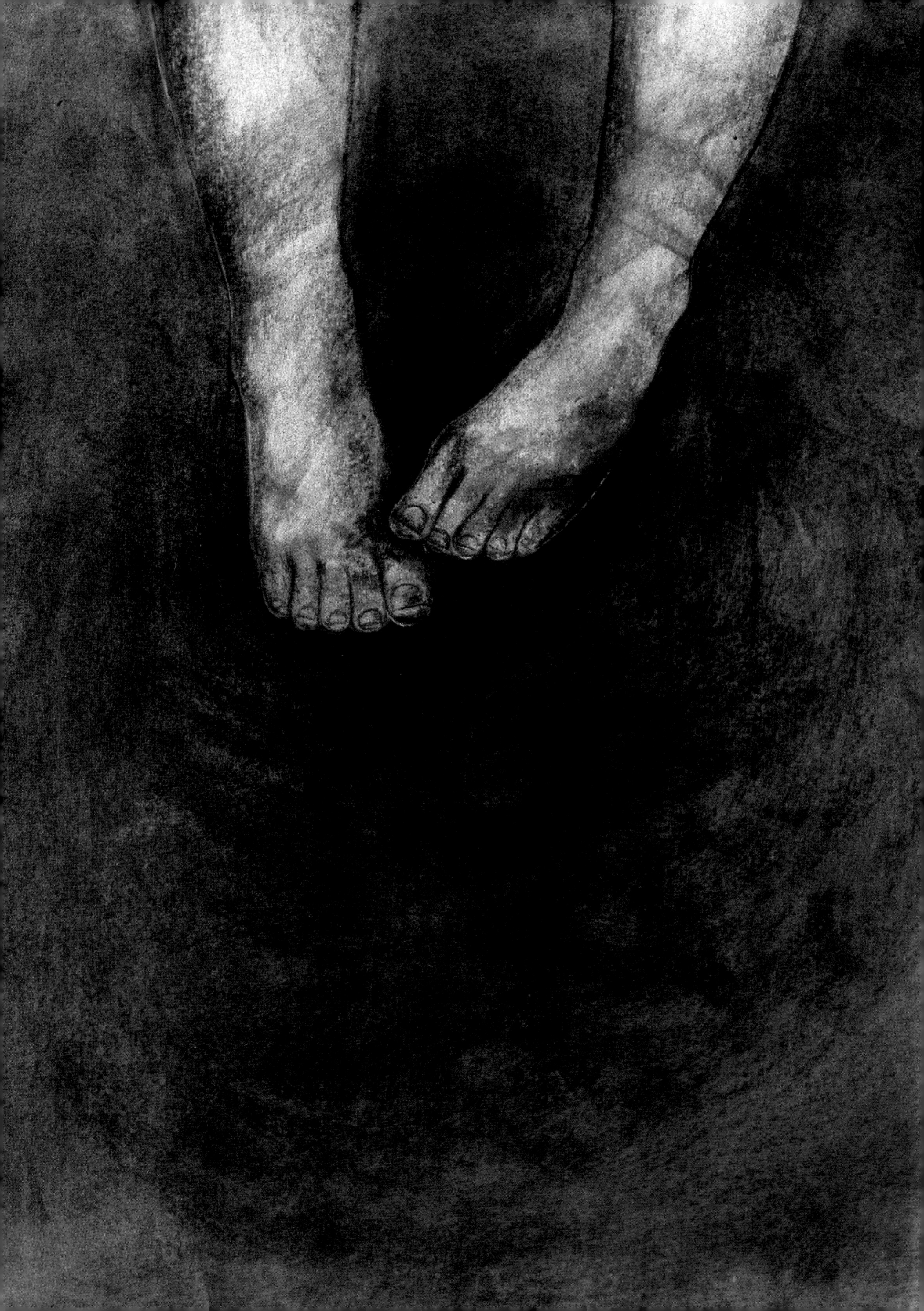

I look at the smooth legs of the models
in the magazines, then I look at mine, filled with scars.

I imagine being a model with scar-filled legs.
I imagine telling people the story behind these scars.

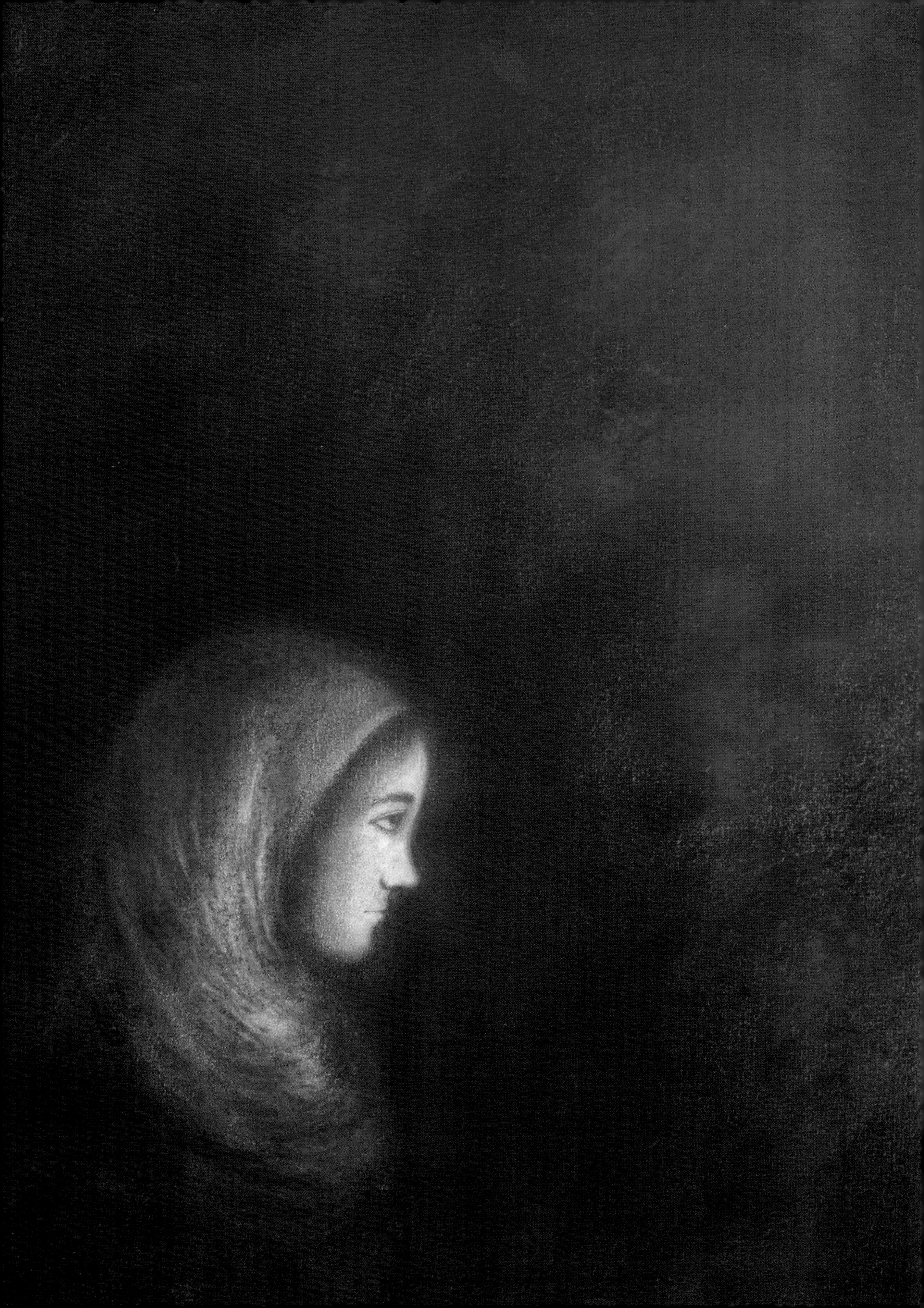

I share my deepest darkest secrets with the night sky
in my window. Some nights are particularly bright.

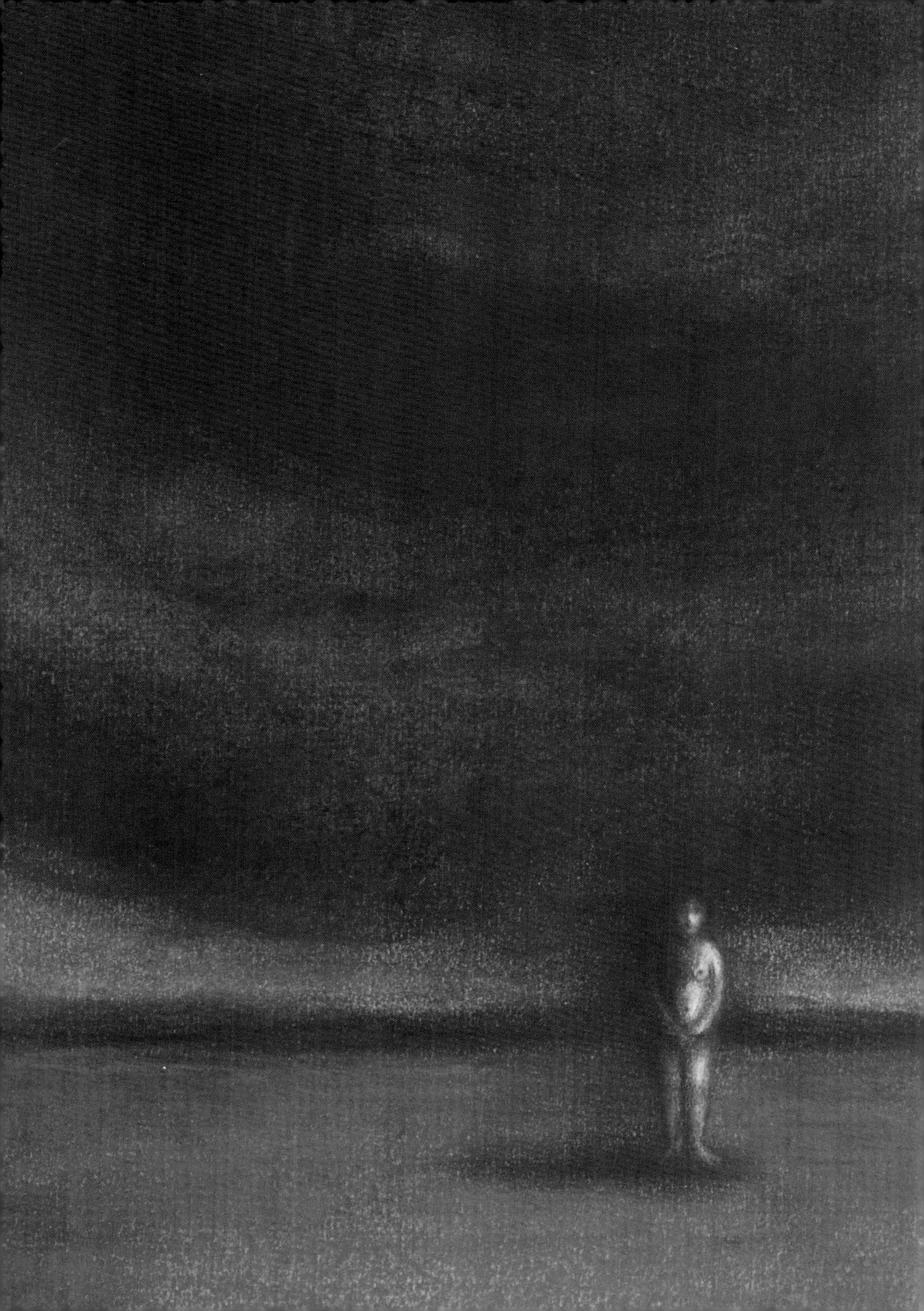

My old clothes don't fit me any more.

Sometimes I feel like I am shrinking.

Like no one can see me.

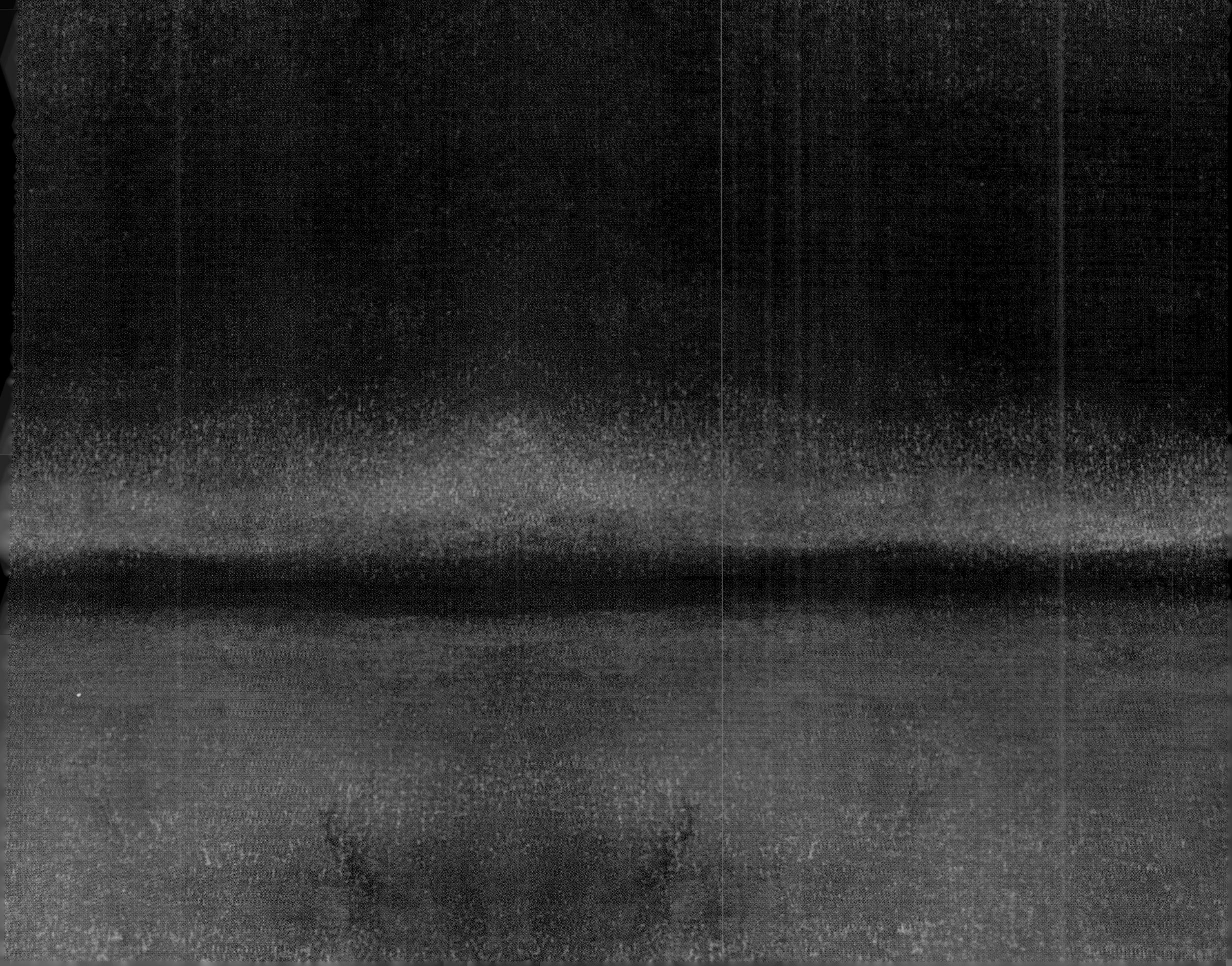

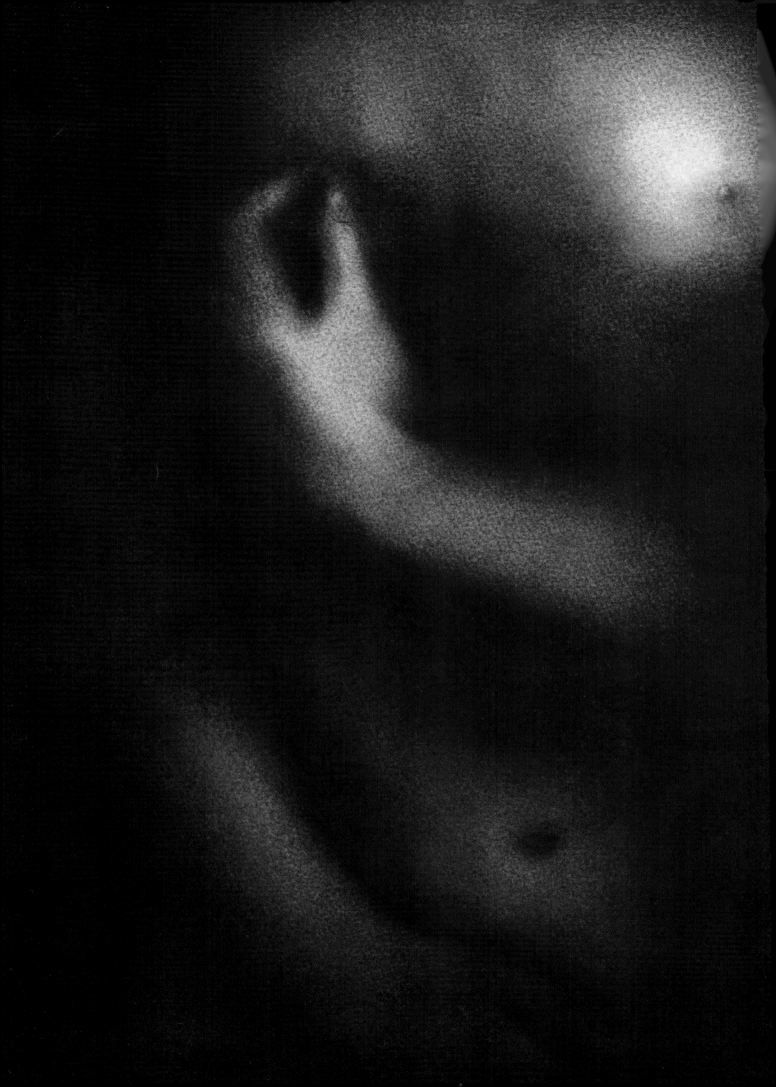

Sometimes at night I touch my new, growing body.
It's full of surprises, happy ones, scary ones.

Just like some days in my town are full of surprises,
happy ones, scary ones.

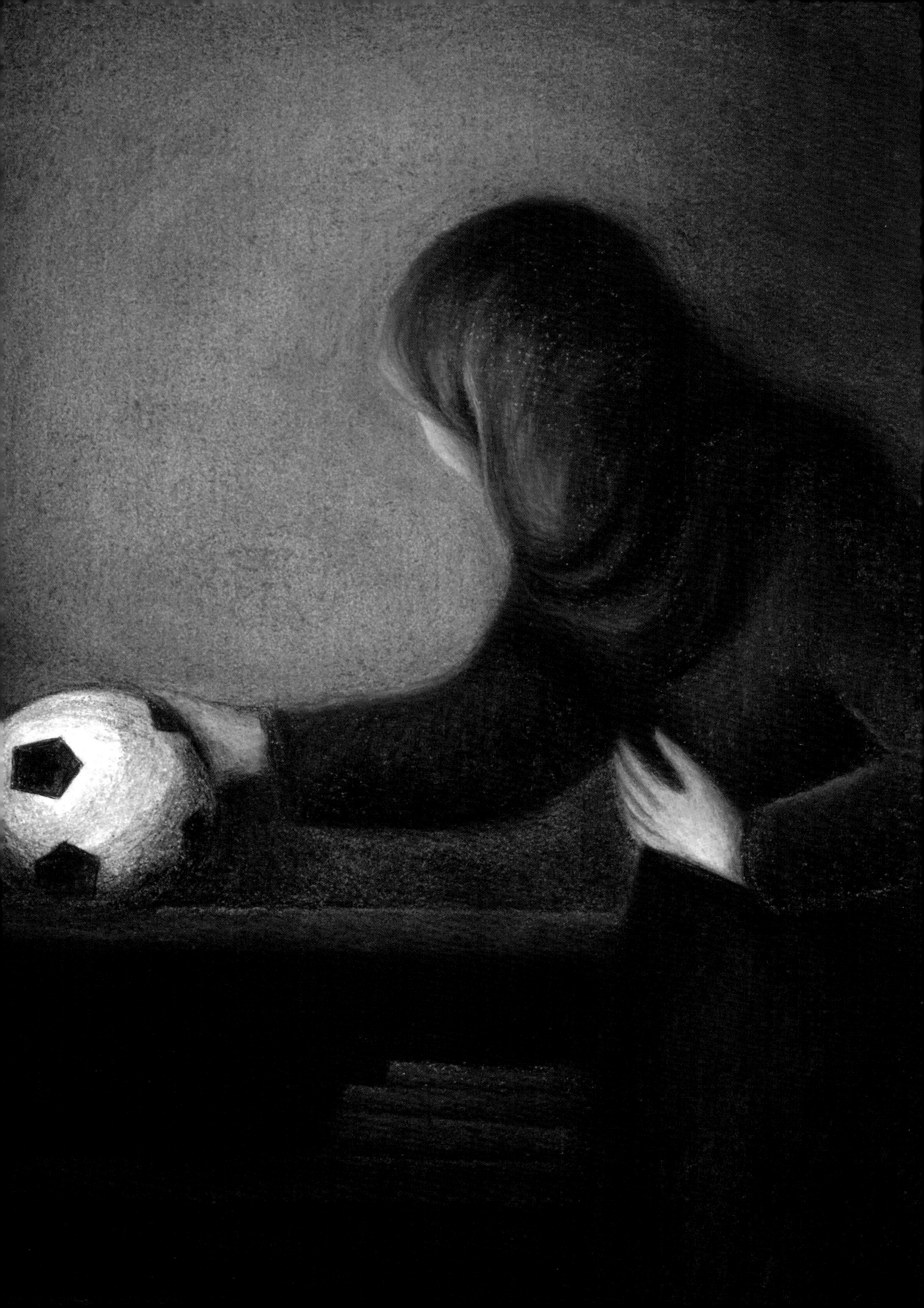

Sometimes I sneak into my brother's room and fool around with his stuff. Mother has kept everything for when he returns.

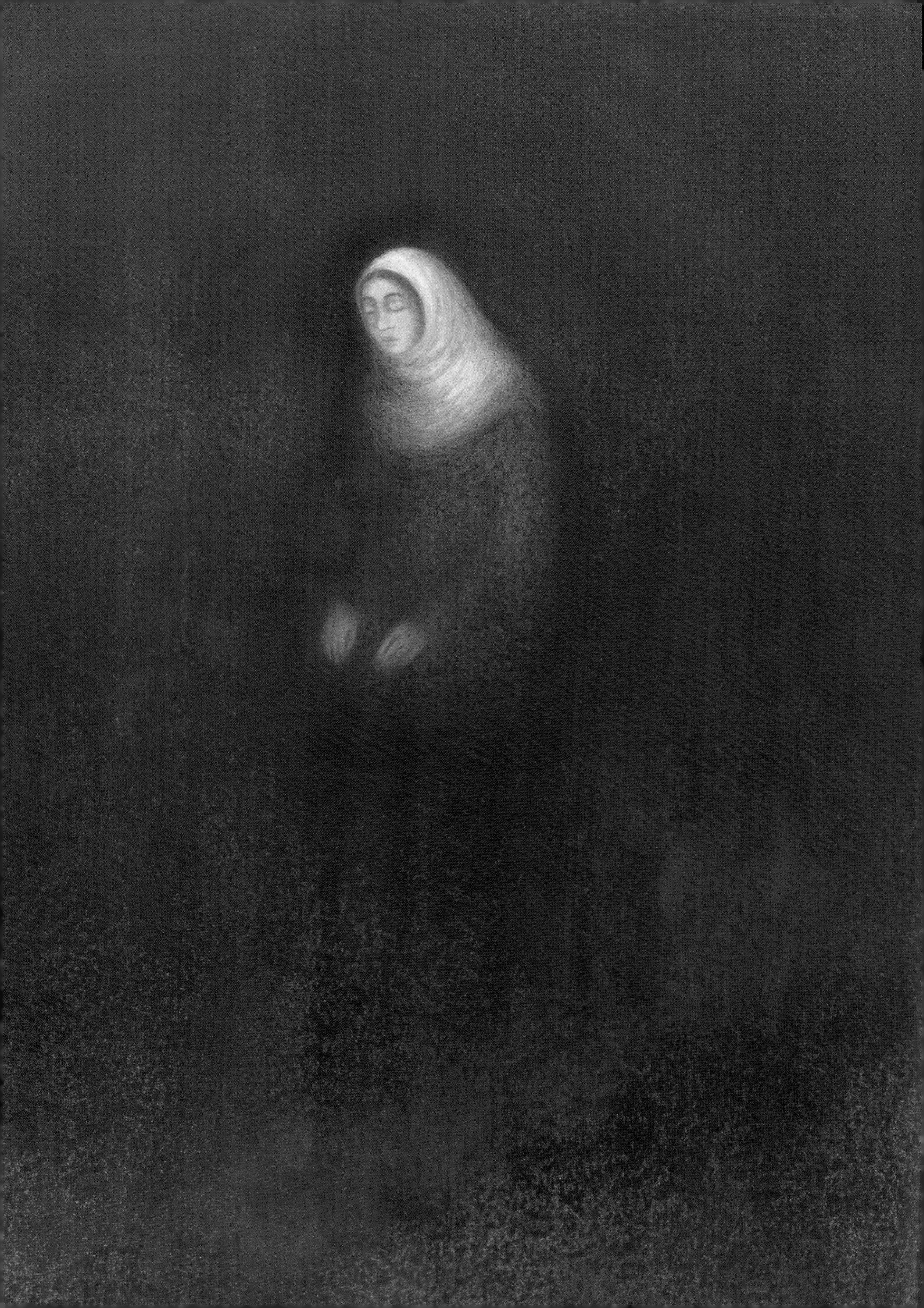

My moods are so confusing these days.
I don't feel like crying when everyone in the town is.
I cry sometimes in the privacy of my room.


And I laugh sometimes, for no good reason.

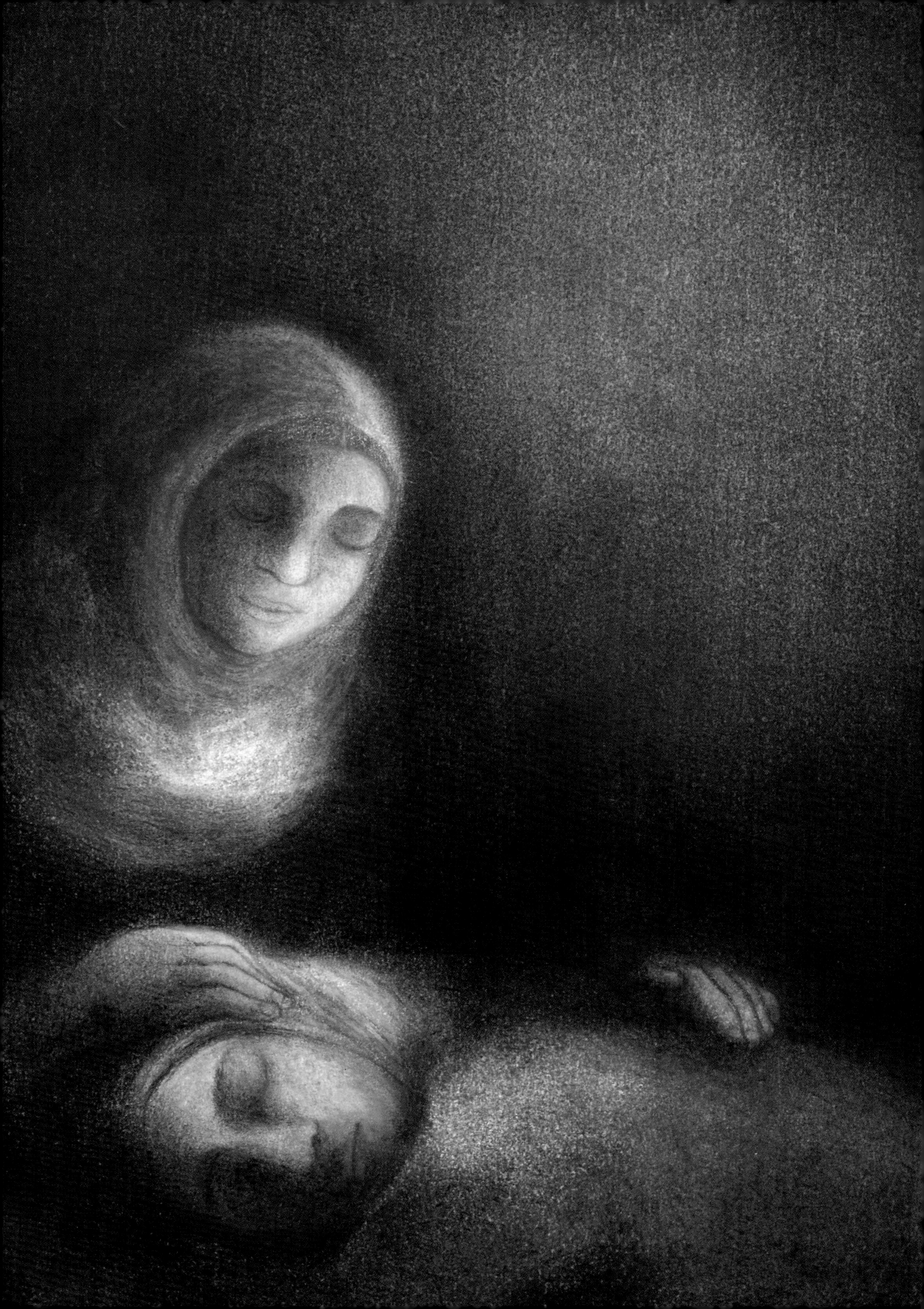

Last night, Mother put her head in my lap and slept.
I hummed a lullaby for her.
I felt like a grown-up.
Like I am a mother too.

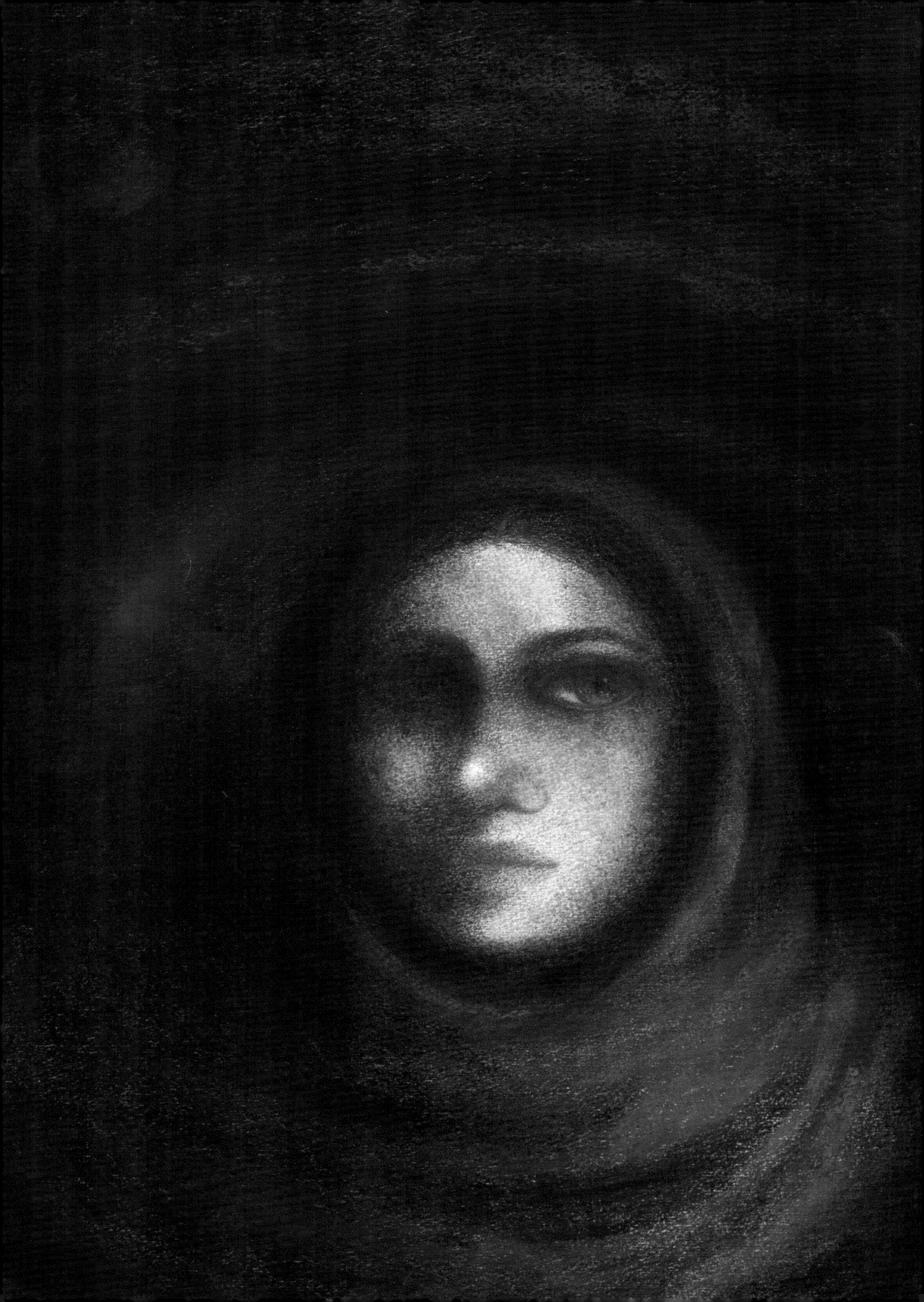